For Mom, who teaches us everyday what strength looks like.
Hannah

First published in the United Kingdom in 2021 by Lantana Publishing Ltd.
www.lantanapublishing.com | info@lantanapublishing.com

American edition published in 2021 by Lantana Publishing Ltd., UK.

Text © Hannah Carmona, 2021
Illustration © Anna Cunha, 2021

The moral rights of the author and illustrator have been asserted.

Distributed in the United States and Canada by Lerner Publishing Group, Inc.
241 First Avenue North, Minneapolis, MN 55401 U.S.A.
For reading levels and more information, look for this title at www.lernerbooks.com
Cataloging-in-Publication Data Available.

Printed and bound in the United States.
Original artwork using mixed media, finished digitally.

Hardcover ISBN: 978-1-911373-63-6
PDF eBook ISBN: 978-1-911373-69-8
Trade ePub3 ISBN : 978-1-913747-60-2
S&L ePub3 ISBN: 978-1-913747-47-3

ANITA
AND THE
DRAGONS

Hannah Carmona
Anna Cunha

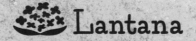 Lantana

Today is the day I will meet the dragons—
large winged beasts who will carry me away.
For years, I have watched the dragons
high above me as I play, hopping from one
cement roof to another. Their snarls shake
the gravel roads.

But being the valiant *princesa* I am, I never
let them scare me!

"They aren't real dragons," my brother Juan reminds me.
"They're just planes in the sky."

"Humph," I say. "Leave my palace at once. You servants
can be such a nuisance."

"We don't live in a palace!" my older brother Tony retorts.

"Of course *you* don't! I, *Princesa* Anita, would never
allow a toad like you inside my walls."

It may not be a real palace, and they may not be real dragons, but I will always be a real *princesa* here on my island. With my trusty steed, and delicious *arroz con leche*, all my royal subjects adore me.

So they are extremely sad when I tell them I will be meeting the ferocious dragons today. With their muscles so strong, they will swoop my entire family and me away—taking us to live on a distant land far, far away from the Dominican Republic.

"*Princesa*, our new palace will have hot water and a real dryer," says Mami, as she dances with Abuela to *merengue* music. I move to the beat, giddy at the thought of a warm bath.

Abuela is not coming, so we must tell her every detail. We promise to send thousands of pictures. Both she and I are sad. However, like a brave *princesa*, I hold her hand and give her my brightest smile each time we talk about the new palace.

"We'll learn English, and the government will not turn off the electricity every night," Mami rambles over the sing-song chant of the *vendedor*. I nod along, imagining an evening reading by lamp light instead of gas lamps.

"But where will *Princesa* Anita receive steaks as fine as mine?" the butcher asks.

Mami's voice, fast and loud, fills the tiny shop as she speaks of all the stores we will live near. There will even be restaurants with staff who wait upon us!

It is a bumpy ride to the dragons' lair. Twice we stop
for another car to pass.

My eyes are wet from having said goodbye to my
trusty steed and Abuela. My usually happy stomach
feels as though someone is squeezing it too tightly.
But, like a brave *princesa*, I hold my chin high.

It is time to meet the dragons.

The rumble of the beasts roars all around
the hot, crowded airport. Sweat drips down
my back. My steps feel heavier than usual.
Papi leads the way.

Face to face with the massive beast,
my throat clenches. Wings protrude from
either side. Eyes line the slender body.
Already the beast hums in anticipation.

The surrounding dragons take flight,
flying so high that soon they are nothing
more than a speck, small enough to pinch
between my fingers.

Courageously, passengers move towards the dragon.
But not me. Not this *princesa*.

I look up at Papi and Mami. "I won't let this horrible
beast take me away from everything I love! What if
I hate it? What if I'm lonely? What if I get scared?
What if I'm sad? What if I'm NOT brave at all?"

No one speaks. Mami touches her rosary beads. The clammy hands of my brothers grip my own. Papi's shifting eyes settle downward.

I am not the only one who will miss my island. I close my eyes. I swallow hard. A rock the size of my fist presses down my throat before it lands with a plunk in the empty pit of my stomach.

I breathe in the sea salt-drenched air deeply. I send a silent message to my island. A message filled with mango-sweet kisses; black, stormy nights; glassy, blue waves; spicy, hot heat—and sandy, snug hugs. I will see you again.

With one step, I move away from the familiar.
With another step, I walk into the unknown.
Hand in hand, we stand strong. Bravely,
through the dark, narrow throat of the beast,
we enter its belly where we will take flight to
new adventures.

I am no longer a watcher of dragons.
I am a fearless dragon of my own.